What Can You Do

With a Rebozo?

by Carmen Tafolla
Illustrations by Amy Córdova

TRICYCLE PRESS
BERKELEY

Text copyright © 2008 by Carmen Tafolla
Illustrations copyright © 2008 by Amy Córdova

All rights reserved. Published in the United States by Tricycle Press, an imprint
of the Crown publishing Group, a division of Random House, Inc, New York.
www.crownpublishing.com
www.tricyclepress.com

Tricycle Press and the Tricycle Press colophon
are registered trademarks of Random House, Inc.

Library of Congress Cataloging-in-Publication Data

Tafolla, Carmen. 1951-
What Can You Do with a Rebozo? / by Carmen Tafolla.
p. cm.
Summary: A spunky, young Mexican American girl explains the
many uses of her mother's red rebozo, or long scarf.
1. Mexican Americans--Juvenile literature. [1. Mexican Americans--Fiction.
2. Scarves--Fiction. 3. Stories in rhyme.] I. Title.
PZ8.3.T114915 Wh 2007
[E]--dc22
2006039624

ISBN 978-1-58246-220-2

Printed in China.
Design by Katie Jennings
Typeset in Mother Hen and Adriatic
The illustrations in this book were rendered in acrylic on paper.

12 11 10 9 8 7 6 5 4 3

First Edition

What can you DO with a rebozo?

Mama spreads it like a butterfly to
pretty up her dress for Sunday morning...

or wraps it into a cozy cradle for
baby brother, so her hands are free...

to weave a braid for me!

Baby brother ducks under a rebozo to play hide-and-seek!

And do a peekaboo peek!

Big sister twirls a rebozo 'round and 'round
and ropes it through her shiny hair.

Grandma uses hers to keep
the cold away on winter nights.

It's nice and warm in there!

Yesterday, Tío wiped up a spill
with Mama's blue rebozo.

And I helped, too!

It was full of sticky, red ketchup spots,
but Daddy washed it clean as new!

On my birthday we swung
a piñata up into the tree
and wound the rebozo over our eyes.

When we burst that big ball of treats
out came a yummy surprise!

You can turn it into a secret tunnel,
if you have two chairs...

or a sash for a pirate at sea!

Or even a flying cape—

and the superhero is ME!

When my puppy didn't feel good,
I made him a bandage, all nicely tied.

And when my cousins turned
my room into a playground,
it became a long, red slide.

But what I like to do most with a rebozo is DANCE!

La Bamba, my favorite dance.

I dance...and dance...

and DANCE with my rebozo.

I swirl and I leap...

until I'm so tired
that I fall fast asleep
on Mama's bed,
where she covers me...

oh so
gently
with her
red
rebozo.

❧ About Rebozos ❧

For centuries, women in Mexico have known that a rebozo (pronounced reh-bóh-soh), or Mexican shawl, can be remarkably handy. Rebozos are used for everything from dressing up for a party to carrying firewood. A rebozo can become a quick umbrella, a beautiful cape to swirl at a village folk dance, or a sling for parents to carry their babies.

Rebozos are made of the finest silk or everyday cotton. They are woven in factories or sewn by hand. In the old days, some rebozo factories wove real gold threads into their rebozos to make them into very special gifts. Today, many Latina women wear rebozos to weddings, fiestas, and quinceañeras.

❀ What can YOU do with a Rebozo? ❀

What is the silliest thing
you can do with a rebozo?

What is the most practical?

The most beautiful?

The most creative?